鶴　鶴　　鶴　鶴　　鶴　鶴　　鶴

鶴　　　　鶴　　　　鶴　　　　鶴

鶴　鶴　　鶴　鶴　　鶴　鶴　　鶴

鶴　　　　鶴　　　　鶴　　　　鶴

鶴　鶴　　鶴　鶴　　鶴　鶴　　鶴

鶴　　　　鶴　　　　鶴　　　　鶴

鶴　鶴　　鶴　鶴　　鶴　鶴　　鶴

鶴　　　　鶴　　　　鶴　　　　鶴

鶴　鶴　　鶴　鶴　　鶴　鶴　　鶴

鶴　鶴　　鶴　鶴　　鶴　鶴　　鶴　鶴

　鶴　　　　鶴　　　　鶴　　　　鶴

鶴　鶴　　鶴　鶴　　鶴　鶴　　鶴　鶴

　鶴　　　　鶴　　　　鶴　　　　鶴

鶴　鶴　　鶴　鶴　　鶴　鶴　　鶴　鶴

　鶴　　　　鶴　　　　鶴　　　　鶴

鶴　鶴　　鶴　鶴　　鶴　鶴　　鶴　鶴

　鶴　　　　鶴　　　　鶴　　　　鶴

鶴　鶴　　鶴　鶴　　鶴　鶴　　鶴　鶴

Copyright © 2000 by Nord-Süd Verlag AG, Gossau Zürich, Switzerland
First published in Switzerland under the title *Der Herr der Kraniche—Ein chinesische Sage*
English translation © 2000 by North-South Books Inc.
All rights reserved. No part of this book may be reproduced
or utilized in any form or by any means, electronic or mechanical,
including photocopying,recording, or any information storage and
retrieval system, without permission in writing from the publisher.
First published in the United States, Great Britain, Canada,
Australia, and New Zealand in 2000 by North-South Books,
an imprint of Nord-Süd Verlag AG, Gossau Zürich, Switzerland.
First paperback edition published in 2002 by North-South Books.
Distributed in the United States by North-South Books Inc., New York.

A CIP catalogue record for this book is available from The British Library.
Library of Congress Cataloging-in-Publication Data
Chen, Kerstin.
[*Herr der Kraniche*. English]
Lord of the cranes: a Chinese tale / retold by Kerstin Chen;
illustrated by Jian Jiang Chen; translated by J. Alison James.
p. cm.
"A Michael Neugebauer book."
Summary: To test the compassion of the people in the city, the lord of the cranes leaves
his home high in the mountains and travels there disguised as a beggar,
but only one man, the innkeeper, passes the test.
[1. Folklore—China.] I. Chen, Jian Jiang, ill. II. James, J. Alison. III. Title.
PZ8.1.C3957 Lo 2000   398.2'0951'0452832   [E]—dc21   99-57811

ISBN 0-7358-1192-X (trade edition) 10 9 8 7 6 5 4 3 2 1
ISBN 0-7358-1193-8 (library edition) 10 9 8 7 6 5 4 3 2 1
ISBN 0-7358-1699-9 (paperback edition) 10 9 8 7 6 5 4 3 2 1
Printed in Italy

For more information about our books, and the authors and artists
who create them, visit our web site: www.northsouth.com

LORD OF
THE CRANES

A CHINESE TALE
Retold by Kerstin Chen
Illustrated by Jian Jiang Chen
Translated by J. Alison James

A Michael Neugebauer Book
NORTH-SOUTH BOOKS / NEW YORK / LONDON

There are places in China where the mountains reach all the way up to the clouds. High up on one of these mountains lived a wise old man. His name was Tian, which means "heaven."

There among the clouds lived Tian's friends, the cranes. Tian fed them and cared for them. The birds told Tian of the wonders they had seen on their flights down below. Tian was devoted to these birds, and they would do anything for him. That is why Tian was called Lord of the Cranes.

One day Tian decided to go down to the city. He wanted to see if people were remembering to be kind and generous. So the old man settled himself on the back of a crane and flew through the clouds.

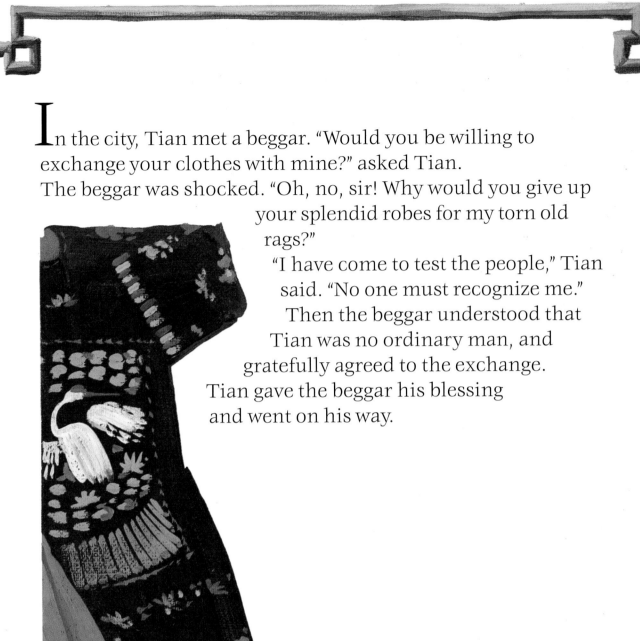

In the city, Tian met a beggar. "Would you be willing to exchange your clothes with mine?" asked Tian.
The beggar was shocked. "Oh, no, sir! Why would you give up your splendid robes for my torn old rags?"
"I have come to test the people," Tian said. "No one must recognize me."
Then the beggar understood that Tian was no ordinary man, and gratefully agreed to the exchange. Tian gave the beggar his blessing and went on his way.

Day after day, Tian went begging through the streets of the beautiful city. Many wealthy people passed by, but no one seemed to even notice him. Not a single person dropped a coin in Tian's cup.

One evening Tian arrived, tired and hungry, at a small inn. Wang, the owner, welcomed him, "What can I do for you?"

"Could you give me a little something to eat and drink?" asked Tian. "I'm sorry, but I have no money to pay."

Wang smiled cheerfully and waved away the apology.

Sit down. Take a rest!" Wang brought the old man a warm bowl of soup, rice, tea, and a plate of sizzling meat. Tian's heart was as full as his belly when he left the inn that evening.

On the following evening, Tian stood again at Wang's door.
"Please, sir, could I have a sip of rice wine and a bite of Joa-tze to eat?" he asked.
"My pleasure, and don't worry about the cost," answered Wang.
Tian ate and drank, and smiled his thanks.
From then on, Tian came every day to Wang's inn, where he was always welcome.

Many months went by in this way. One day, Tian said to Wang, "I am deeply in your debt. You have been so good to me, I must find a way to repay you." Wang was quite surprised. "But you do not need to repay me! What I have given to you, I've given gladly. It makes me happy when I can help someone." Tian smiled. "Nonetheless, I would like to repay you. Of course, I have no money, but I can give you something else. . . ."

Tian untied a gourd from his walking stick. It looked like a water flask, but Tian used it like the finest sable brush to paint a picture of three cranes on the wall of the inn. Wang was astonished. "It is wonderful!" he exclaimed. "Heavenly!"

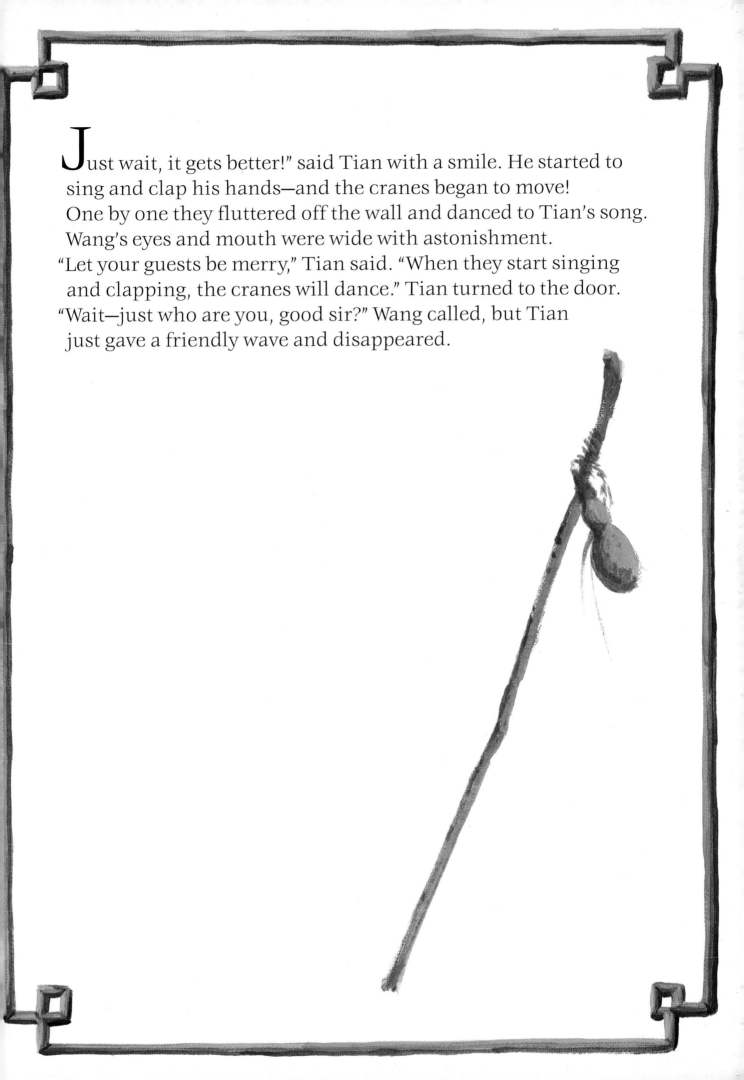

J ust wait, it gets better!" said Tian with a smile. He started to
sing and clap his hands—and the cranes began to move!
One by one they fluttered off the wall and danced to Tian's song.
Wang's eyes and mouth were wide with astonishment.
"Let your guests be merry," Tian said. "When they start singing
and clapping, the cranes will dance." Tian turned to the door.
"Wait—just who are you, good sir?" Wang called, but Tian
just gave a friendly wave and disappeared.

Soon everyone in the city was talking about the wondrous dancing cranes at Wang's inn. More and more people came every day to marvel at the beautiful birds.

Before long, Wang was one of the richest men in the city,
but he always kept a seat free and a bowl of soup ready for
anyone in need.

One day Tian returned. Wang hurried to greet him, sat him at the best table, and brought him a delicious meal.

"Please tell me who you are," he begged.

Tian didn't answer. Instead, he lifted his flute to his lips and played a melody that was so tender and beautiful it brought tears to Wang's eyes.

"That was a melody from heaven," whispered Wang. "I thank you for allowing me to hear it. You have made me a rich and happy man. How can I ever repay you?"

"Teach others to be as kind and generous to the poor as you have been to me," said Tian.

"That is my only wish."

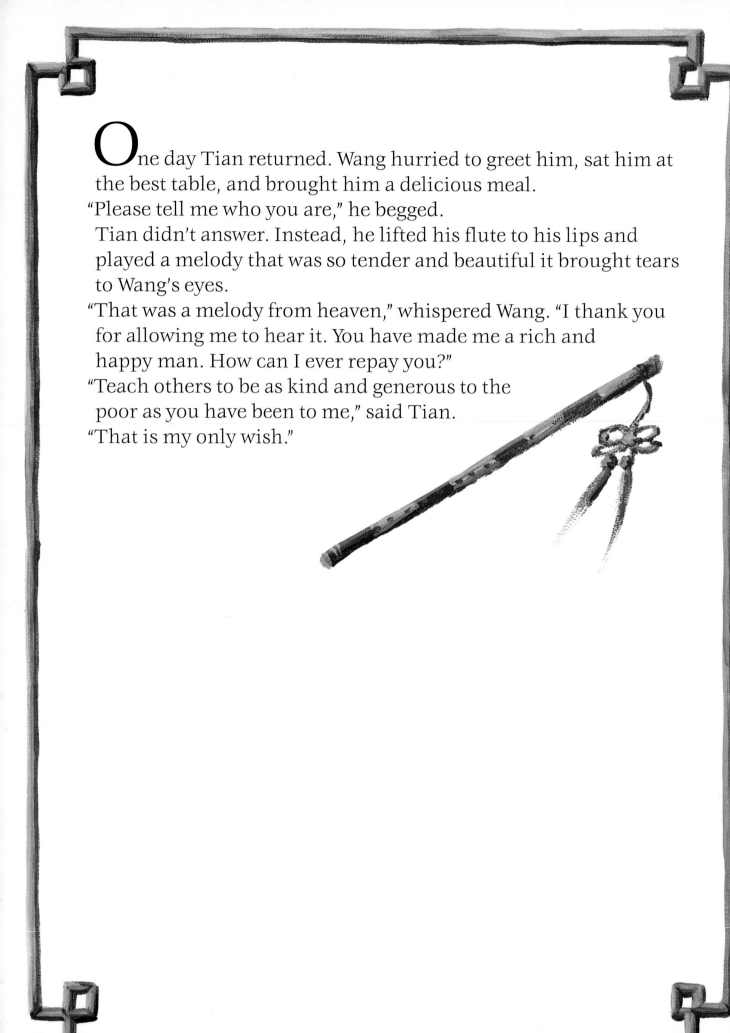

Tian raised the flute to his lips and played the melody from heaven one last time.

The three cranes stepped off the wall and knelt before him. Tian stroked them and said, "I thank you for your help, my friends. We will now fly home." He bowed to Wang. "Farewell, good sir."

Tian flew on the back of one of the cranes, up away from the city and into the sky. A great flock of cranes accompanied them. Wang stood watching the sky long after Tian and the cranes had disappeared.

At last he knew who the unusual beggar really was. Deeply humbled, Wang returned to his inn. For the rest of his life, Wang tried to fulfill the Lord of the Cranes's wish—telling all who would listen of his miraculous encounter with the beggar in disguise and urging them to share with those less fortunate.

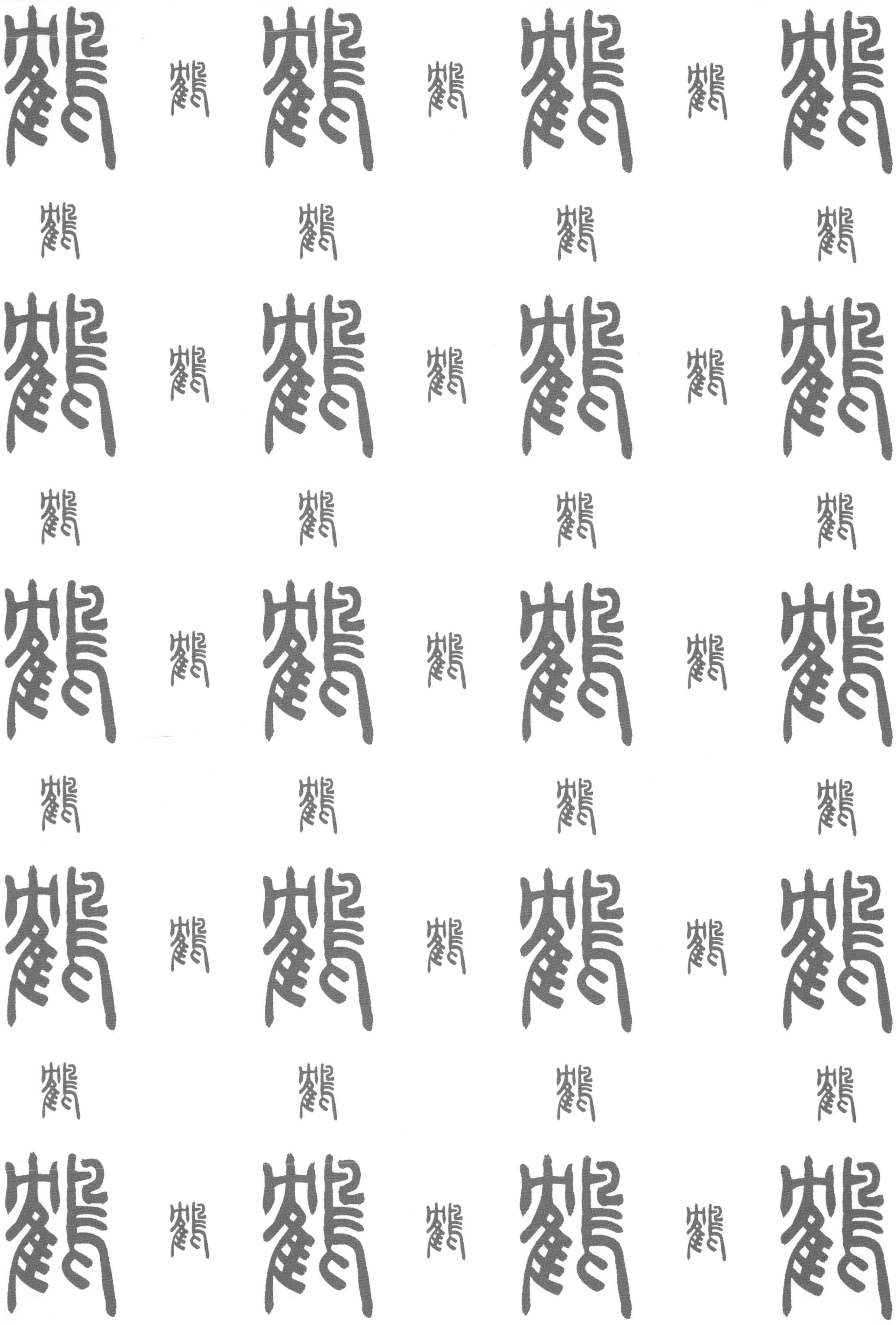

鶴　鶴　鶴　鶴　鶴　鶴　鶴
鶴
鶴　鶴　鶴　鶴　鶴　鶴　鶴
鶴
鶴　鶴　鶴　鶴　鶴　鶴　鶴
鶴
鶴　鶴　鶴　鶴　鶴　鶴　鶴
鶴
鶴　鶴　鶴　鶴